Illustrations by Duendes del Sur

Published by Ladybird Books Ltd 2011
A Penguin Company
Penguin Books Ltd, 80 Strand, London, WC2R 0RL, UK
Penguin Books Australia Ltd, Camberwell, Victoria, Australia
Penguin Group (NZ), 67 Apollo Drive, Rosedale, North Shore 0632, New Zealand
(a division of Pearson New Zealand Ltd)

ISBN: 978 1 409 30948 2

Printed in Slovakia

Scooby and Shaggy were heading to Paris to meet up with the rest of the Mystery, Inc. gang.

"Like, shouldn't we be there by now?" asked Shaggy.

Little did he know that the plane was miles from their holiday destination.

"We will be landing soon," announced Alphonse LaFleur, a monster-hunter posing as a tour guide.

LaFleur used Scooby Snacks to lure Scooby and Shaggy into a crate. Then LaFleur sealed the crate and tossed it out the plane's cargo doors. Suddenly, Scooby and Shaggy were free-falling toward Mount Everest! "Like, elevator going down!" cried Shaggy.

Shaggy and Scooby were racing down the mountainside when Shaggy's mobile phone rang. It was Fred calling from Paris!

Fred tracked Shaggy and Scooby's location using the GPS on his mobile phone. "This can't be right!" cried Fred.
"The Himalayas?" exclaimed Velma. "Home to Mount Everest and the mysterious Abominable Snowman? We've got to rescue them!"

Scooby and Shaggy's wild ride came to an end inside the gates of a monastery. Professor Jeffries, an archaeologist searching for the lost city of Shangri-La, and his Nepalese mountain guide, Pemba, found them.

"Are you alright?" asked Professor Jeffries.

"Yeah, but the rest of the gang must be worried sick about us," cried Shaggy.

Pemba agreed to take Scooby and Shaggy to the weather station. "You can call your friends from there," he said.

"I'll come, too," added the Professor. "It's dangerous out there with the snow creature."

"*Row* reature?" yelped Scooby-Doo. "Rikes!"

The Professor told them about the Abominable Snowman, also known as the *Yeti*.

AHOOOOOH!

Pemba's little sister Mina caught up with the expedition. "There's a storm coming!" she warned.

While everyone settled in for the night, the Professor sneaked off with his supplies. It wasn't long before the Yeti let loose a spine chilling howl.

"Not to worry, I am the greatest monster hunter in all the world!" said LaFleur.

It turned out that LaFleur had tricked Shaggy and Scooby into coming to the Himalayas so that they could be Monster bait for the Abominable Snowman!

"No way, man," cried Shaggy. "You're going to have to bag this winter weirdo on your own!"

Scooby and Shaggy narrowly escaped the Yeti's clutches thanks to the sudden appearance of their old friend, Radio DJ Del Chillman. "I came here months ago to see the monster," said Del, "and I was tired of waiting for him to show up. And now that I'm planning to leave the Himalayas, the Yeti's tracks are everywhere!"

Safely back at the Weather Station where Del was broadcasting from, Shaggy found a strange letter. "Like, hmm . . . I wonder who wrote this strange letter?" he asked Scooby-Doo.

"You two stay here and take over the radio broadcast while I go and search for your friends," instructed Del.

Soon, Fred, Daphne, and Velma arrived at the monastery.

"Check it out gang," added Fred. "Scooby Snacks! And those look like Shaggy and Scooby's tracks!"

"But why would they be heading up the mountain?" asked Daphne.

"I've got a hunch our next clue will be waiting for us in thin air," said Velma. "Let's follow those tracks!"

"There's something strange about these tracks," pondered Velma. "The creature must be huge, but his footprints barely sink into the snow!" Suddenly, Fred saw Pemba in a monster trap, and quickly freed him. "This is my sister Mina's radio!" exclaimed Pemba. "She listens to Del Chillman wherever she goes!"

Unfortunately, the Abominable Snowman listened to the radio too! That's how he found Shaggy and Scooby! After tearing through the Weather Station, the monster chased them up the radio tower.

"You think you can outsmart me, eh beastie?" asked LaFleur, as he threw a net over the Yeti.

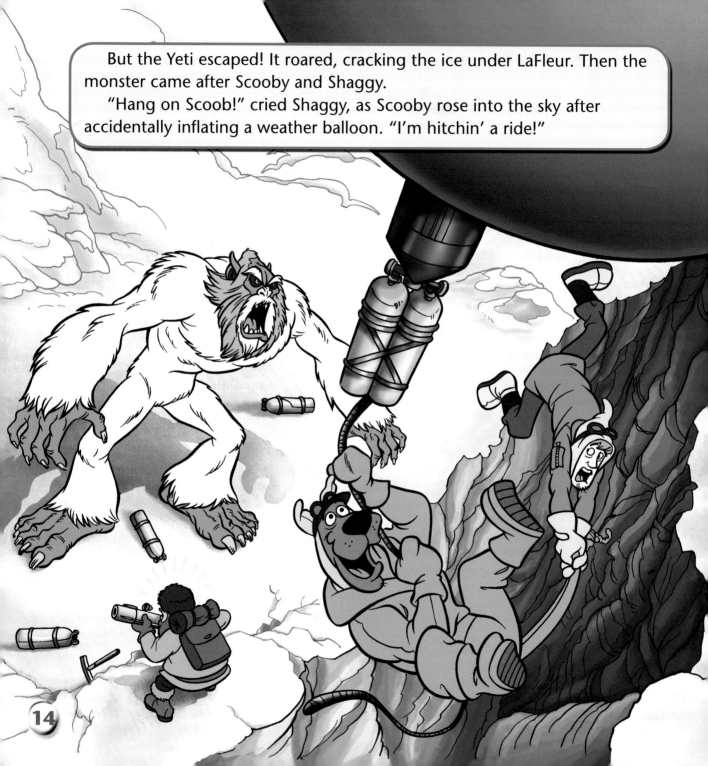

But the Yeti escaped! It roared, cracking the ice under LaFleur. Then the monster came after Scooby and Shaggy.

"Hang on Scoob!" cried Shaggy, as Scooby rose into the sky after accidentally inflating a weather balloon. "I'm hitchin' a ride!"

Velma, Fred, and Del arrived at the Weather Station moments after Scooby and Shaggy floated away.

"According to these inventory records, a few helium tanks are missing," said Velma.

"Take a look at this!" interrupted Del. "This seismograph is picking up some strange vibrations deep inside the mountain!"

"Let's split up to look for clues in the mountain," said Fred.

Scooby and Shaggy dropped from the weather balloon and landed in a secret burial ground.

"Welcome to the lost kingdom of Shangri-La," said the High Lama. "Years ago, men driven by greed came here to seek riches, and our paradise was lost."

"Like, that must be why the snowman has such a chilly personality!" said Shaggy. "He's just trying to protect this place."

Fred and Velma had made their way to the heart of the mountain.
"Jinkies!" cried Velma. "It's an enormous crevice!"

Suddenly, an explosion rocked the very ground they were standing on, uncovering an ancient stone bridge deep in the crevice. Del grabbed some climbing gear from the Snowcat. The three quickly rappelled down to the bridge and headed into the nearest cave entrance.

Meanwhile, Pemba and Daphne were exploring the Yeti's cave. Daphne stubbed her toe on a helium tank.

"What are these doing up here?" asked Pemba.

"I don't know," replied Daphne, "but I think the Abominable Snowman is less snow and more man!"

Suddenly, an explosion revealed another tunnel. "I wonder where it leads?" asked Daphne.

The tunnel in the Yeti's cave led to a crystal cavern. That's where Daphne and Pemba found Del and the rest of the gang. "It's Professor Jeffries!" cried Pemba. "He's trying to steal the sacred crystals!"

KABOOM! Professor Jeffries's blasts loosened the crystals from the cave walls.

"Come on gang!" said Fred. "I've got a plan to catch this crystal craving creep."

While the Professor wasn't looking, Scooby and Shaggy stole his special crystal.

"It all makes sense!" cried Velma. "Professor Jeffries used the legend of the Yeti to scare us away from the mountain so he could steal the . . ."

"I hate to interrupt," gulped Shaggy, pointing to the Yeti who came howling into the cavern. "But, RUN!"

While the Professor and the Yeti chased Scooby, Shaggy and the crystal, the rest of the gang set up an icy trap. Scooby and Shaggy expertly manoeuvred the sledge in the snow. The Professor and the Abominable Snowman came to a crashing halt inside the monastery's gates, where the crystal rolled safely to the High Lama's feet.

The gang wasn't safe yet. At that moment, an avalanche was speeding down the mountainside toward Velma and Del.

"They're not going to make it!" cried Daphne.

Luckily, the Yeti flew into the air and grabbed Velma and Del just in the nick of time.

"A flying Abominable Snowman!" exclaimed Del. "My mind is blown!"

"Try Snow-woman!" cried Velma, as she removed the monster's mask. "Mina used the helium tanks to fill her costume. That's why her footprints didn't sink deeply into the snow."

"I am so sorry," said Mina. "I'm Del's number one fan. When I learned that he was leaving, I brought the Yeti to life so that he would stay."

"That's r-e-a-a-a-l-l c-o-o-o-o-l mama," said Del.

Now that their icy adventure was over, the gang could finally enjoy their holiday!

"Paris is for lovers, right Scoob?" asked Shaggy. "Well I'm in love with this springtime spread!"

Shaggy's mobile phone rang. "Like, hello?" he answered.

"Uh, guys?" said Fred. "I think I got on the wrong plane!"

"Like, next stop, the Amazon Jungle!" cried Shaggy.

Scooby-Dooby-Doo!!!!